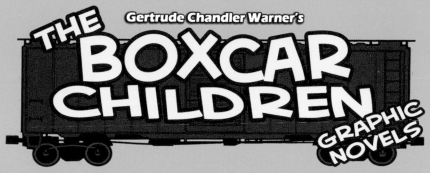

Gertrude Chandler Warner's

THE BOXCAR CHILDREN

GRAPHIC NOVELS

BOOK ONE

THE BOXCAR CHILDREN

Henry, Jessie, Violet, and Benny are a family. They're brothers and sisters—and they're orphans, too. The only way they can stay together is to try and make it on their own. But where will they live?

One night, during a storm, the children find an old red boxcar that keeps them warm and safe. The children decide to make it their home—and they become the Boxcar Children!

THE BOXCAR CHILDREN
GRAPHIC NOVELS

1. THE BOXCAR CHILDREN
2. SURPRISE ISLAND
3. THE YELLOW HOUSE MYSTERY
4. MYSTERY RANCH
5. MIKE'S MYSTERY
6. BLUE BAY MYSTERY

Gertrude Chandler Warner's

THE BOXCAR CHILDREN

Adapted by Shannon Eric Denton
Illustrated by Mike Dubisch

Henry Alden

Watch

Jessie Alden

Violet Alden

Benny Alden

magic
wagon

Visit us at www.abdopublishing.com

Published by Magic Wagon, a division of the ABDO Group, 8000 West 78th Street, Edina, Minnesota 55439. Copyright © 2009 by Abdo Consulting Group, Inc. International copyrights reserved in all countries. All rights reserved. No part of this book may be reproduced in any form without written permission from the publisher. Graphic Planet™ is a trademark and logo of Magic Wagon. This edition produced by arrangement with Albert Whitman & Company. THE BOXCAR CHILDREN is a registered trademark of Albert Whitman & Company. www.albertwhitman.com

Adapted by Shannon Eric Denton
Illustrated by Mike Dubisch
Colored by Wes Hartman
Lettered by Kristen Fitzner Denton
Edited by Stephanie Hedlund
Interior layout and design by Kristen Fitzner Denton
Cover art by Mike Dubisch
Book design and packaging by Shannon Eric Denton

Library of Congress Cataloging-in-Publication Data

Denton, Shannon Eric.
  Boxcar children / adapted by Shannon Eric Denton; illustrated by Mike Dubisch.
     p. cm. -- (Gertrude Chandler Warner's boxcar children)
  ISBN 978-1-60270-586-9
 [1. Orphans--Fiction. 2. Family--Fiction. 3. Mystery and detective stories.] I. Dubisch, Michael, ill. II. Warner, Gertrude Chandler, 1890-1979. Boxcar children. III. Title.
  PZ7.D4373Box 2009
  [E]--dc22
                                        2008036095

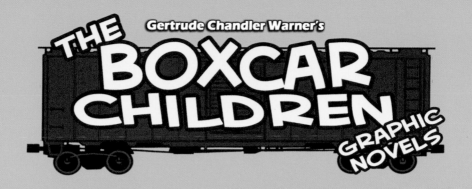

Contents

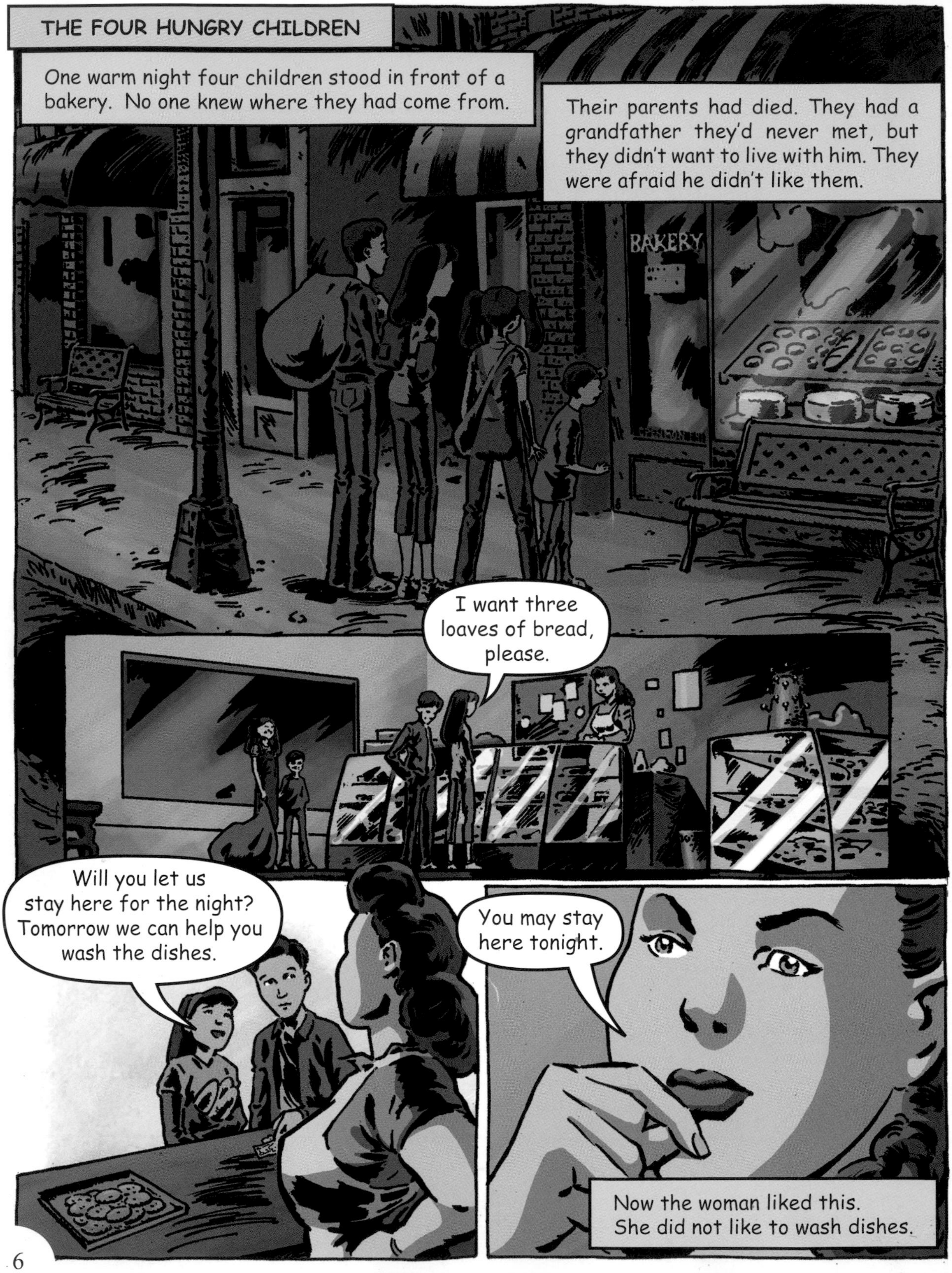

THE FOUR HUNGRY CHILDREN
One warm night four children stood in front of a bakery. No one knew where they had come from.
Their parents had died. They had a grandfather they'd never met, but they didn't want to live with him. They were afraid he didn't like them.
BAKERY
I want three loaves of bread, please.
Will you let us stay here for the night? Tomorrow we can help you wash the dishes.
You may stay here tonight.
Now the woman liked this. She did not like to wash dishes.

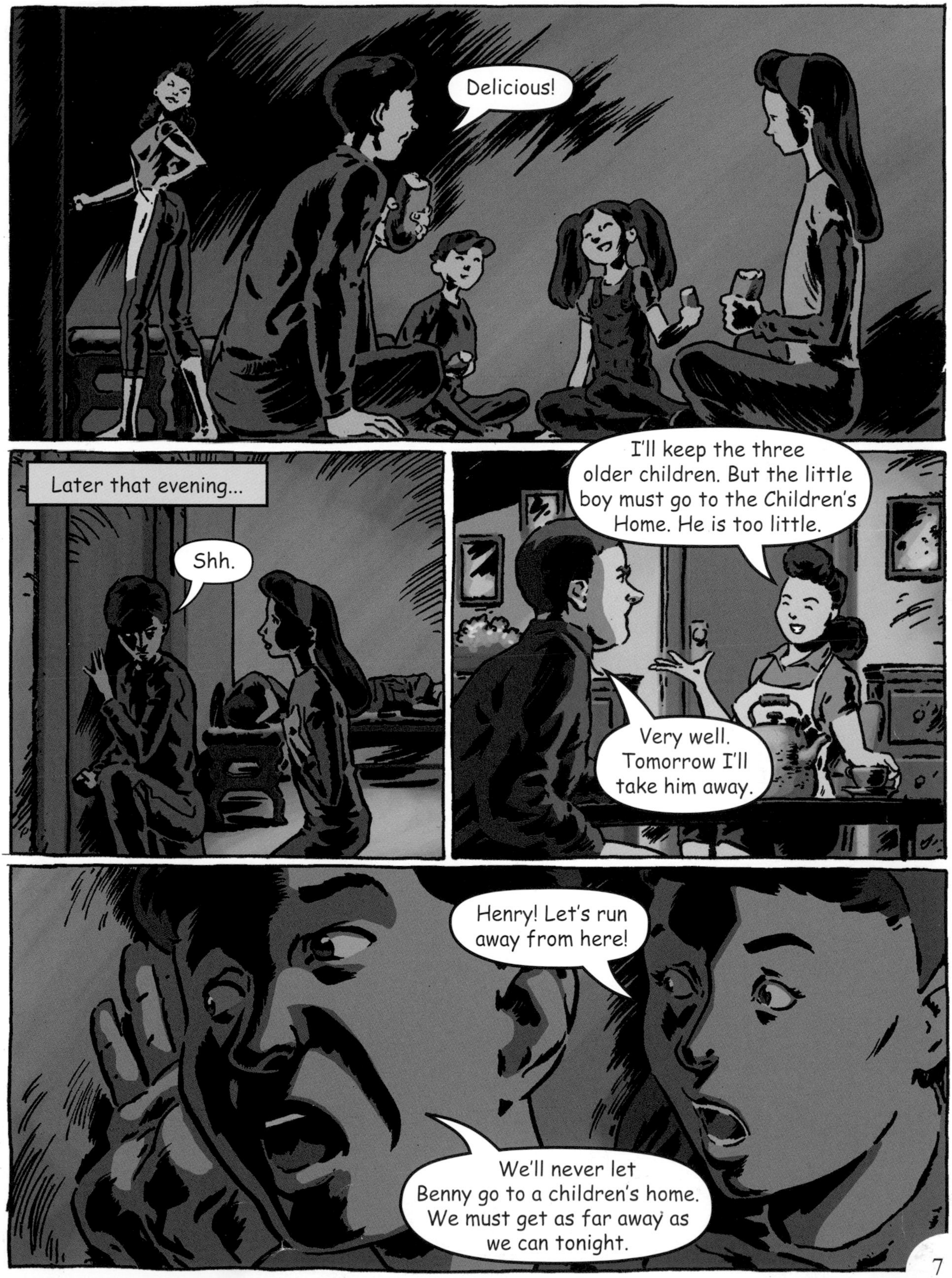
Delicious!
Later that evening...
Shh.
I'll keep the three older children. But the little boy must go to the Children's Home. He is too little.
Very well. Tomorrow I'll take him away.
Henry! Let's run away from here!
We'll never let Benny go to a children's home. We must get as far away as we can tonight.

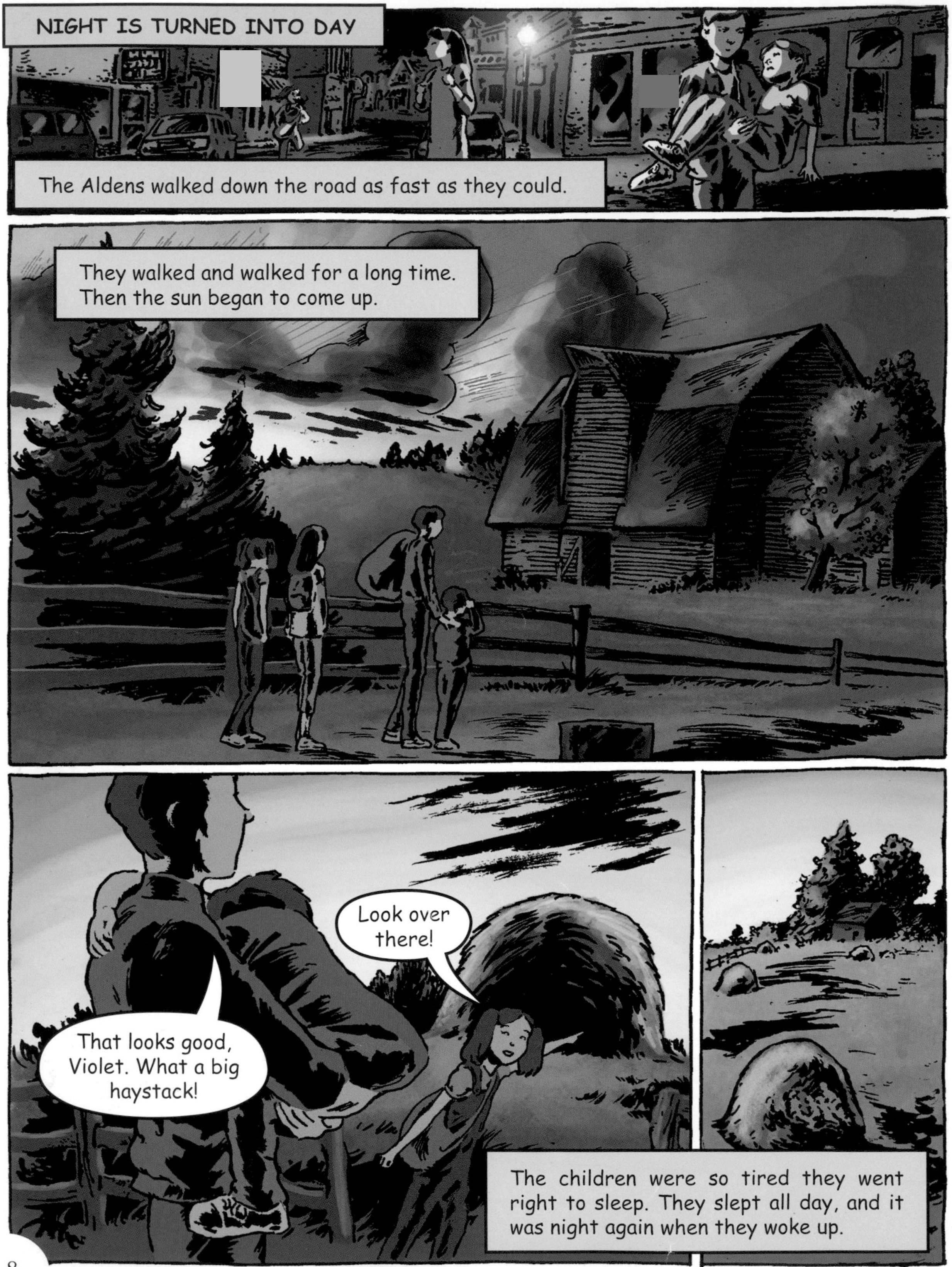

NIGHT IS TURNED INTO DAY
The Aldens walked down the road as fast as they could.
They walked and walked for a long time. Then the sun began to come up.
Look over there!
That looks good, Violet. What a big haystack!
The children were so tired they went right to sleep. They slept all day, and it was night again when they woke up.

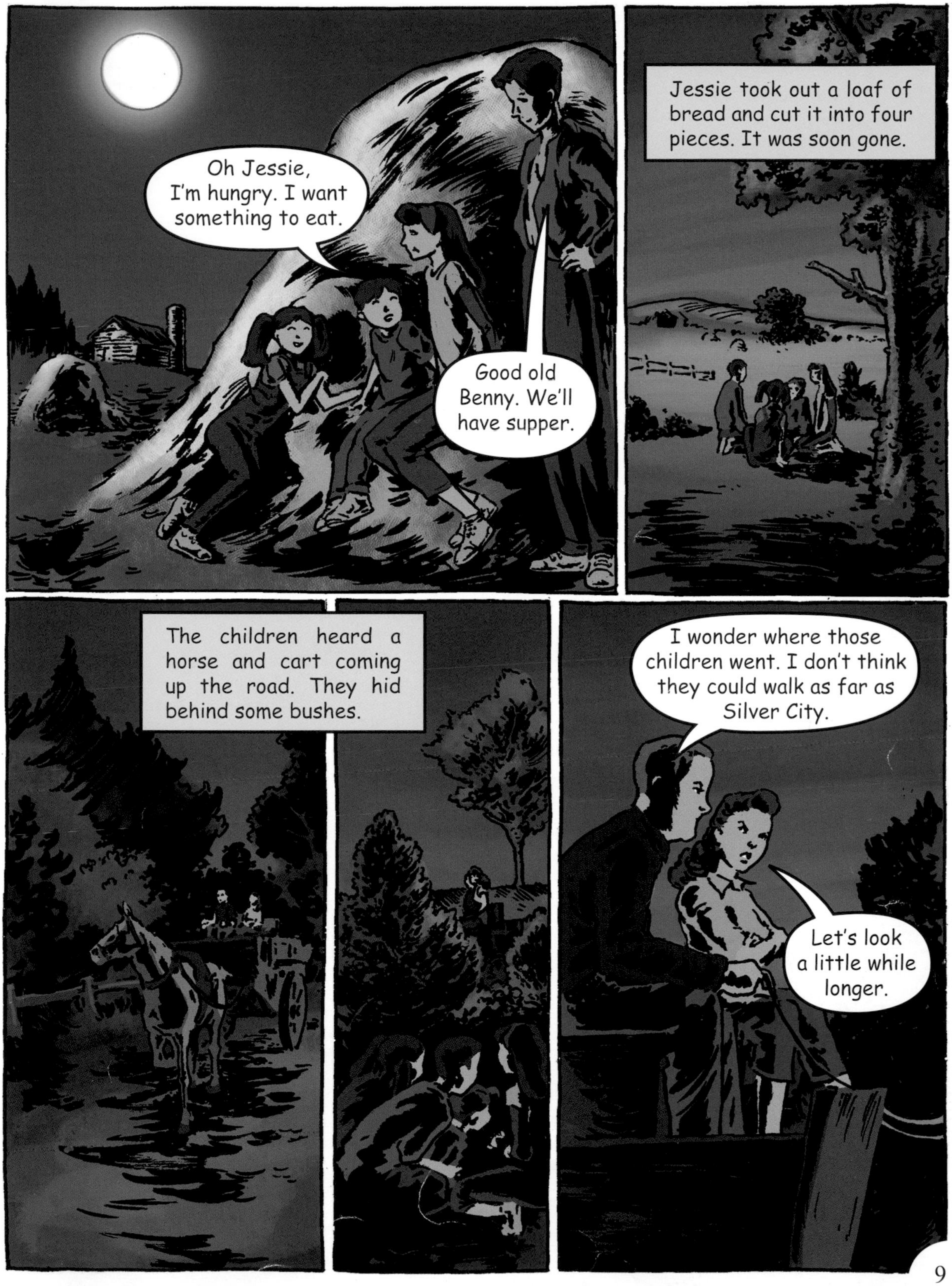
Oh Jessie,
I'm hungry. I want
something to eat.
Good old
Benny. We'll
have supper.
Jessie took out a loaf of
bread and cut it into four
pieces. It was soon gone.
The children heard a
horse and cart coming
up the road. They hid
behind some bushes.
I wonder where those
children went. I don't think
they could walk as far as
Silver City.
Let's look
a little while
longer.

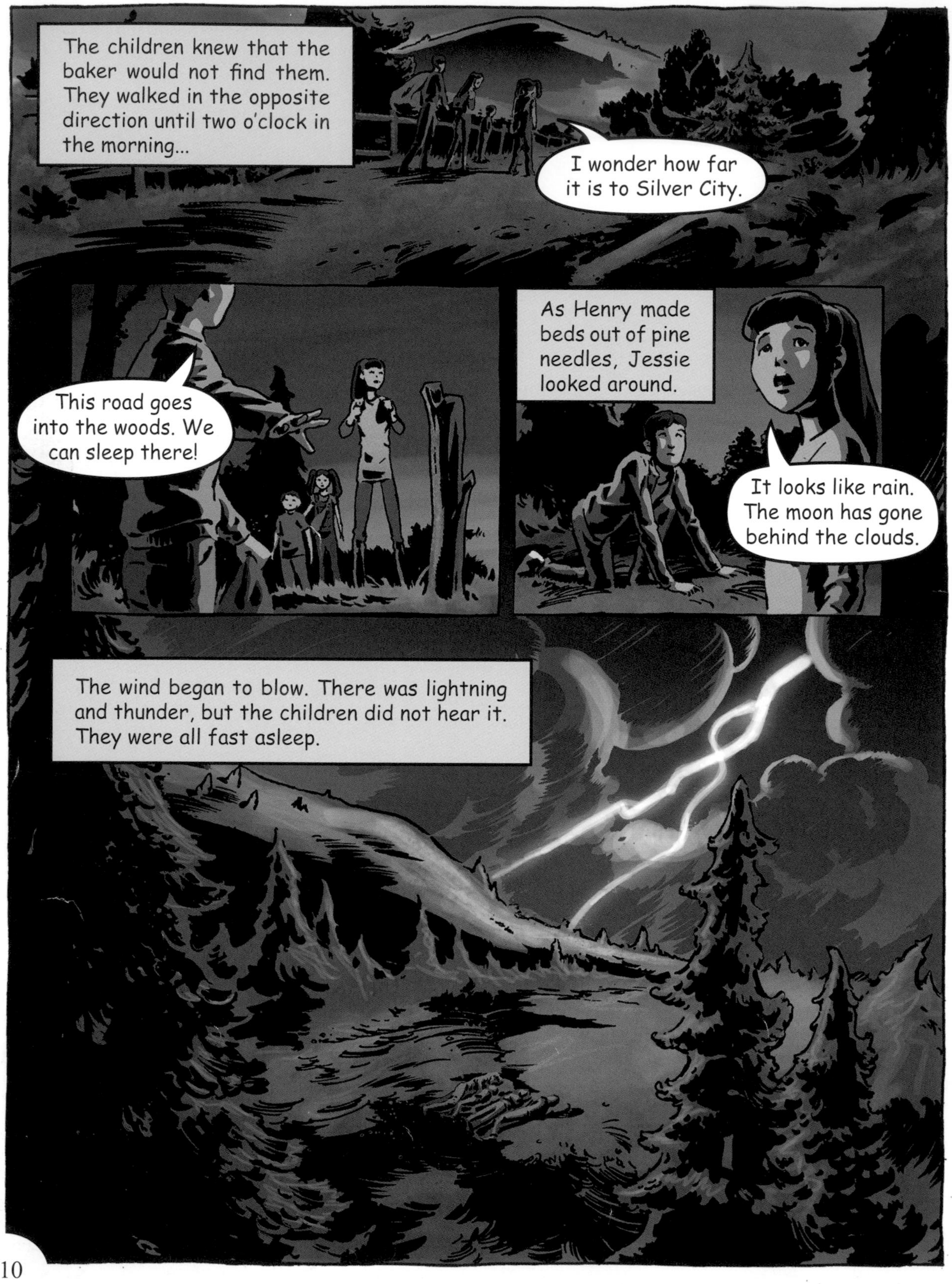
The children knew that the baker would not find them. They walked in the opposite direction until two o'clock in the morning...
I wonder how far it is to Silver City.
This road goes into the woods. We can sleep there!
As Henry made beds out of pine needles, Jessie looked around.
It looks like rain. The moon has gone behind the clouds.
The wind began to blow. There was lightning and thunder, but the children did not hear it. They were all fast asleep.

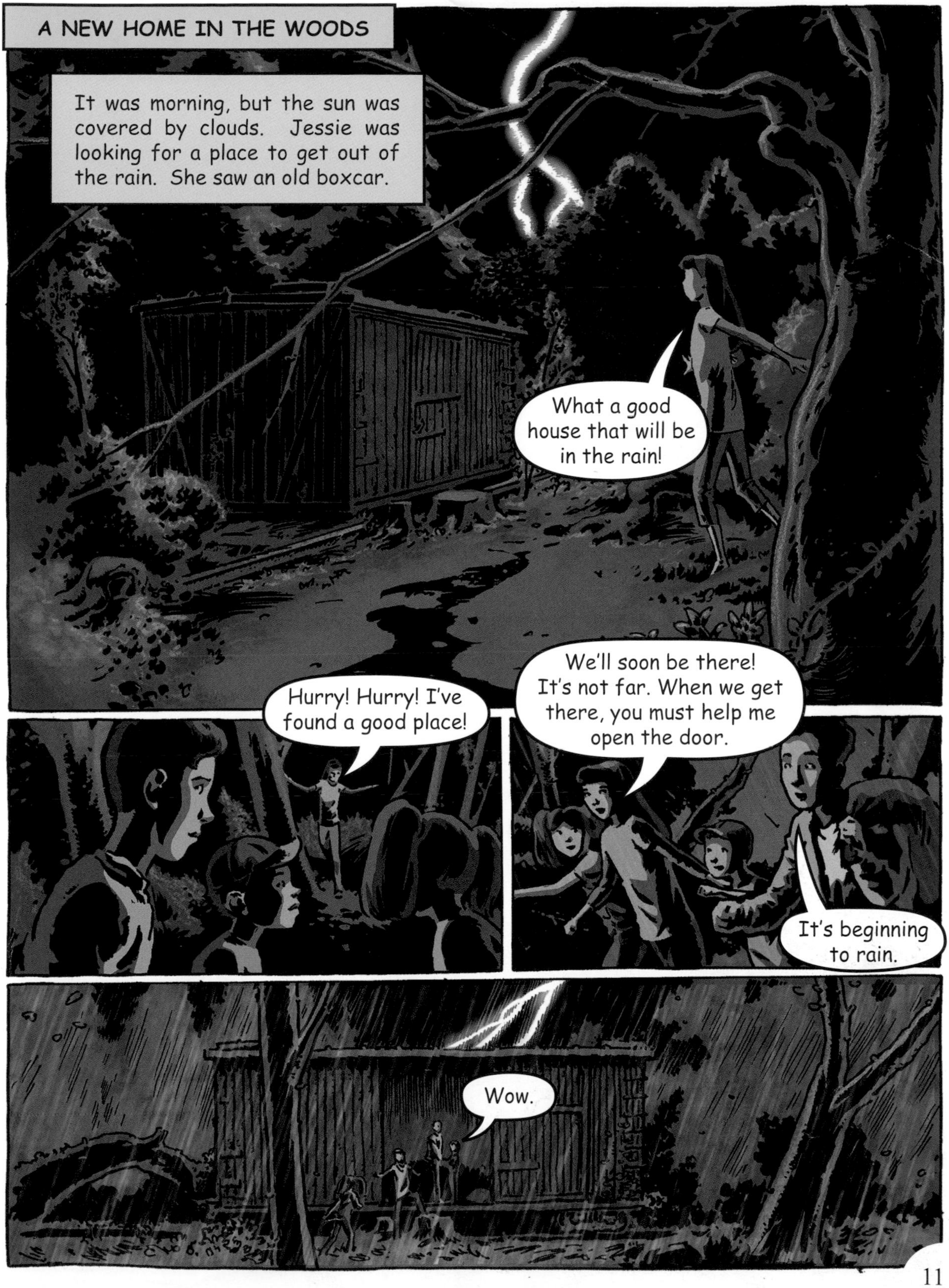
A NEW HOME IN THE WOODS
It was morning, but the sun was covered by clouds. Jessie was looking for a place to get out of the rain. She saw an old boxcar.
What a good house that will be in the rain!
Hurry! Hurry! I've found a good place!
We'll soon be there! It's not far. When we get there, you must help me open the door.
It's beginning to rain.
Wow.

They were just in time. The children could hear the rain on the top of the boxcar, but no rain came in.

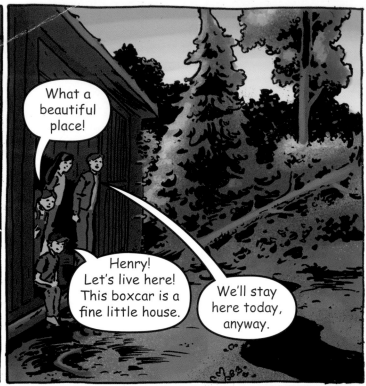

What a beautiful place!

Henry! Let's live here! This boxcar is a fine little house.

We'll stay here today, anyway.

I want some milk.

I'll go to the next town and get some.

Before Henry came back, Jessie heard a noise. Something was in the woods!

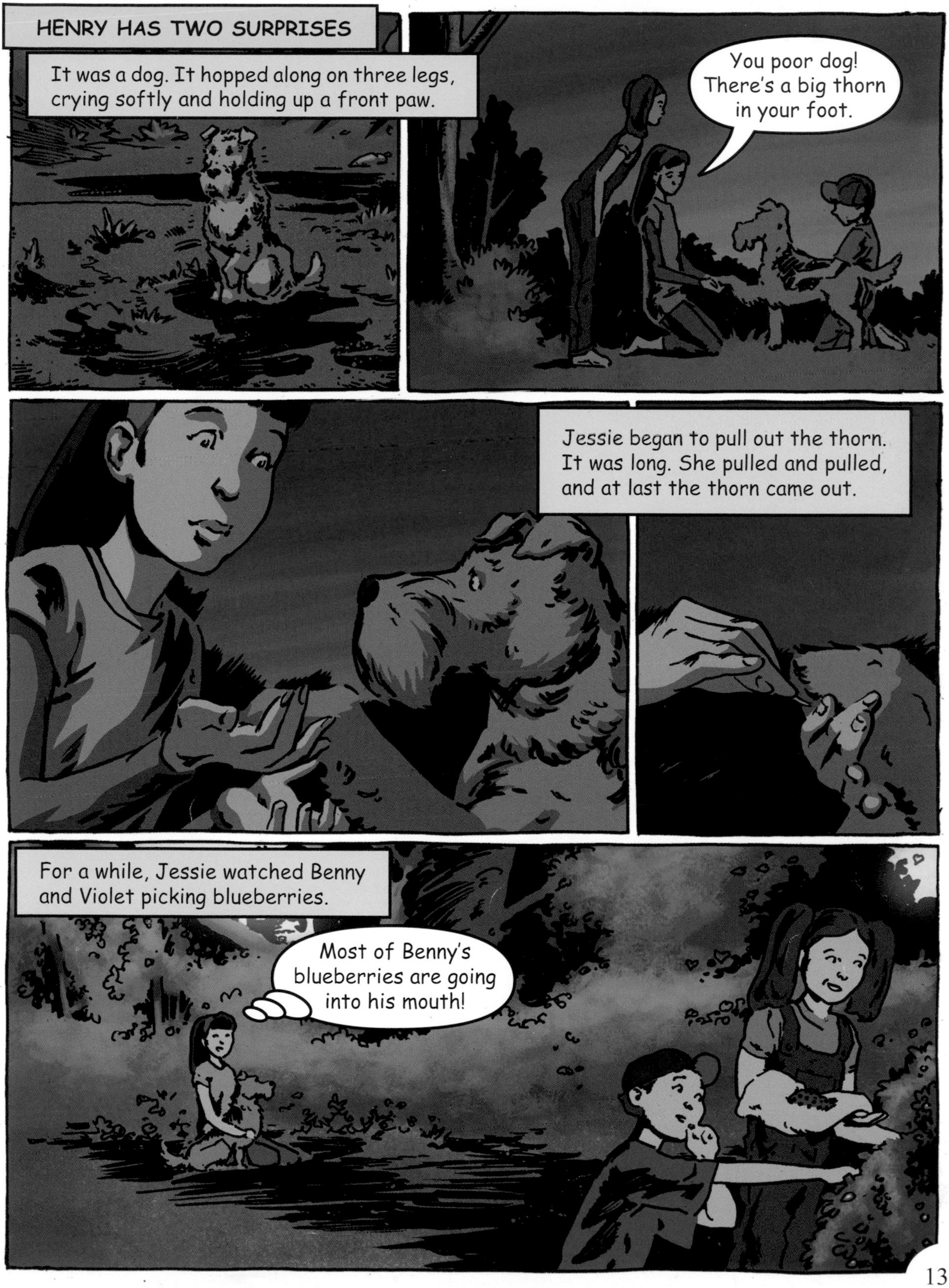
HENRY HAS TWO SURPRISES
It was a dog. It hopped along on three legs, crying softly and holding up a front paw.
You poor dog! There's a big thorn in your foot.
Jessie began to pull out the thorn. It was long. She pulled and pulled, and at last the thorn came out.
For a while, Jessie watched Benny and Violet picking blueberries.
Most of Benny's blueberries are going into his mouth!

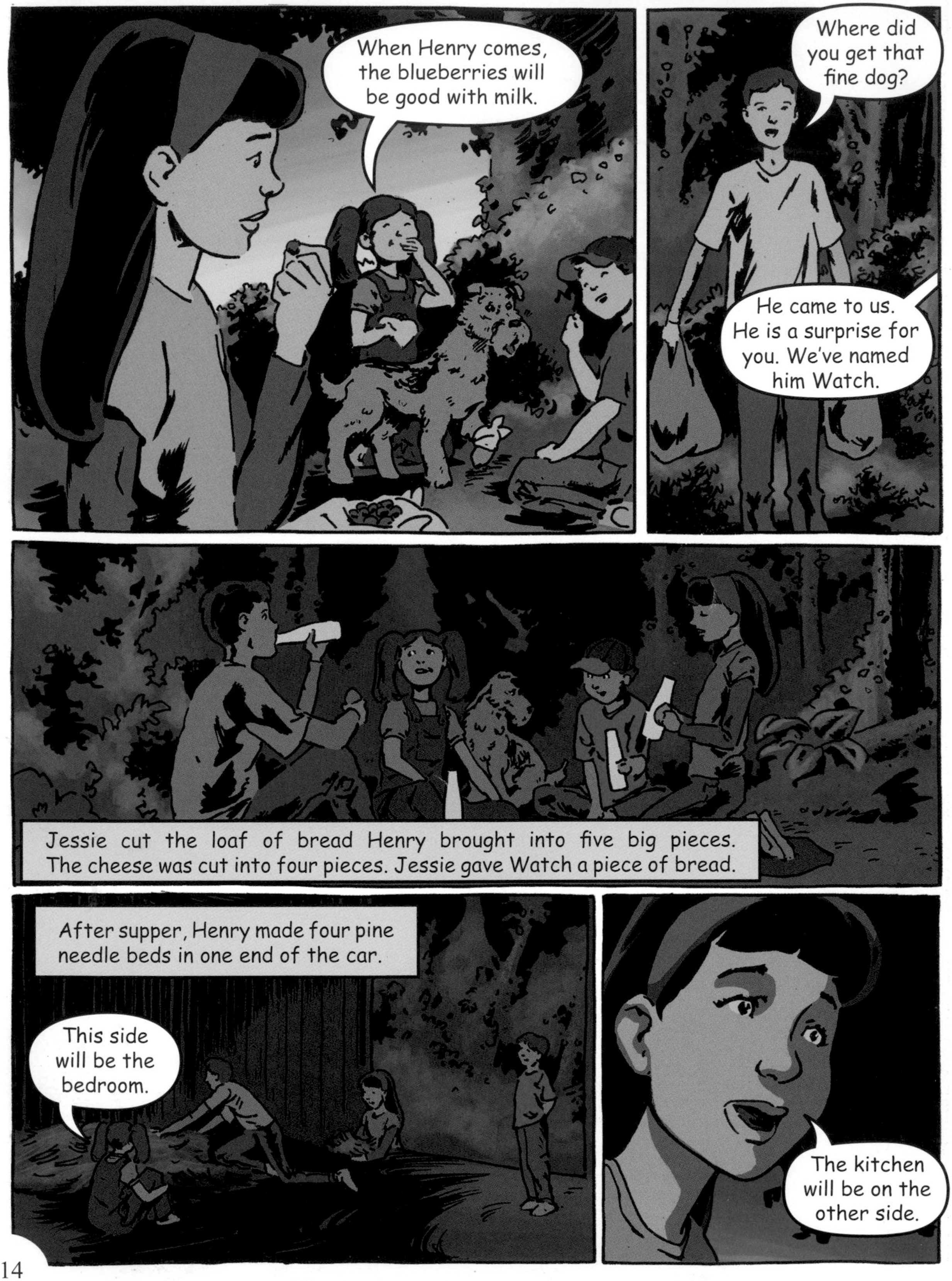
When Henry comes, the blueberries will be good with milk.
Where did you get that fine dog?
He came to us. He is a surprise for you. We've named him Watch.
Jessie cut the loaf of bread Henry brought into five big pieces. The cheese was cut into four pieces. Jessie gave Watch a piece of bread.
After supper, Henry made four pine needle beds in one end of the car.
This side will be the bedroom.
The kitchen will be on the other side.

THE EXPLORERS FIND TREASURE

It looks like home.

Soon they were fast asleep, dog and all. The moon came up but they did not see it. This was the first time in four days that they could go to sleep at night, as children should.

The next morning Jessie woke up first. She got up at once.

I'll go get the milk for breakfast.

Jessie walked down by the little brook and stopped to look at the waterfall. It was beautiful.

Behind the waterfall was a rock. Jessie had put two bottles of milk in a hole in the rock. Now she took them out.

The milk is very cold!

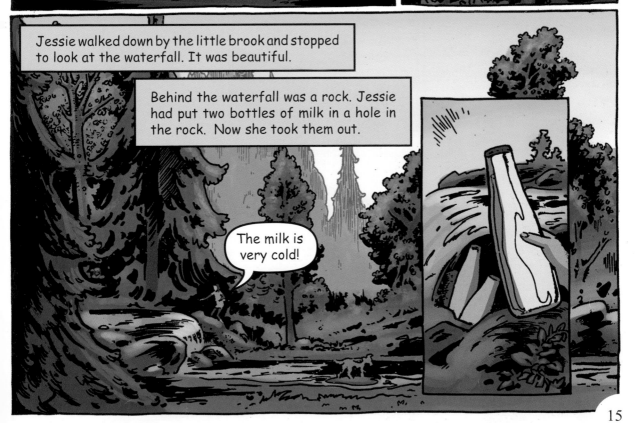

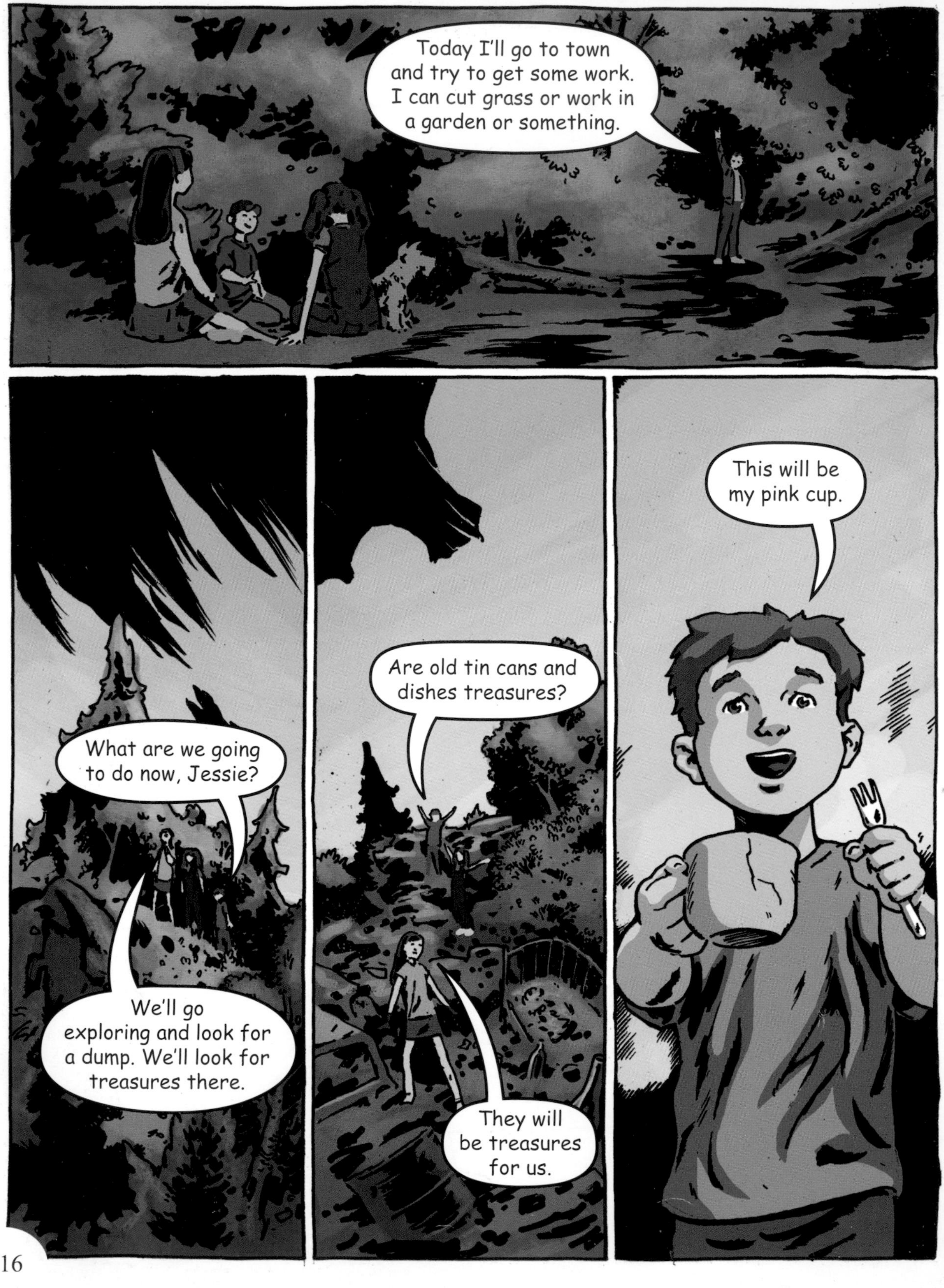
Today I'll go to town and try to get some work. I can cut grass or work in a garden or something.
What are we going to do now, Jessie?
We'll go exploring and look for a dump. We'll look for treasures there.
Are old tin cans and dishes treasures?
They will be treasures for us.
This will be my pink cup.

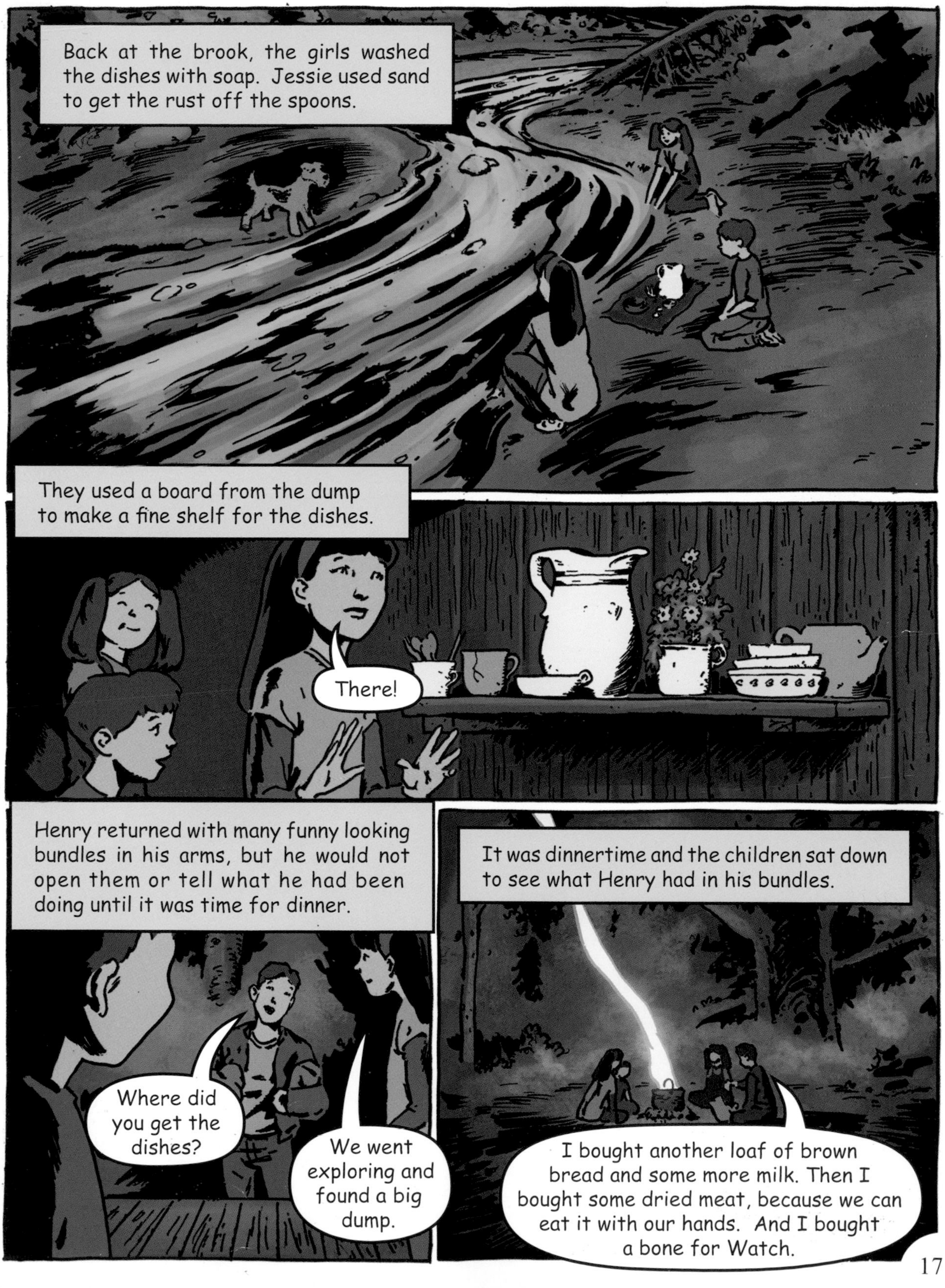
Back at the brook, the girls washed the dishes with soap. Jessie used sand to get the rust off the spoons.
They used a board from the dump to make a fine shelf for the dishes.
There!
Henry returned with many funny looking bundles in his arms, but he would not open them or tell what he had been doing until it was time for dinner.
Where did you get the dishes?
We went exploring and found a big dump.
It was dinnertime and the children sat down to see what Henry had in his bundles.
I bought another loaf of brown bread and some more milk. Then I bought some dried meat, because we can eat it with our hands. And I bought a bone for Watch.

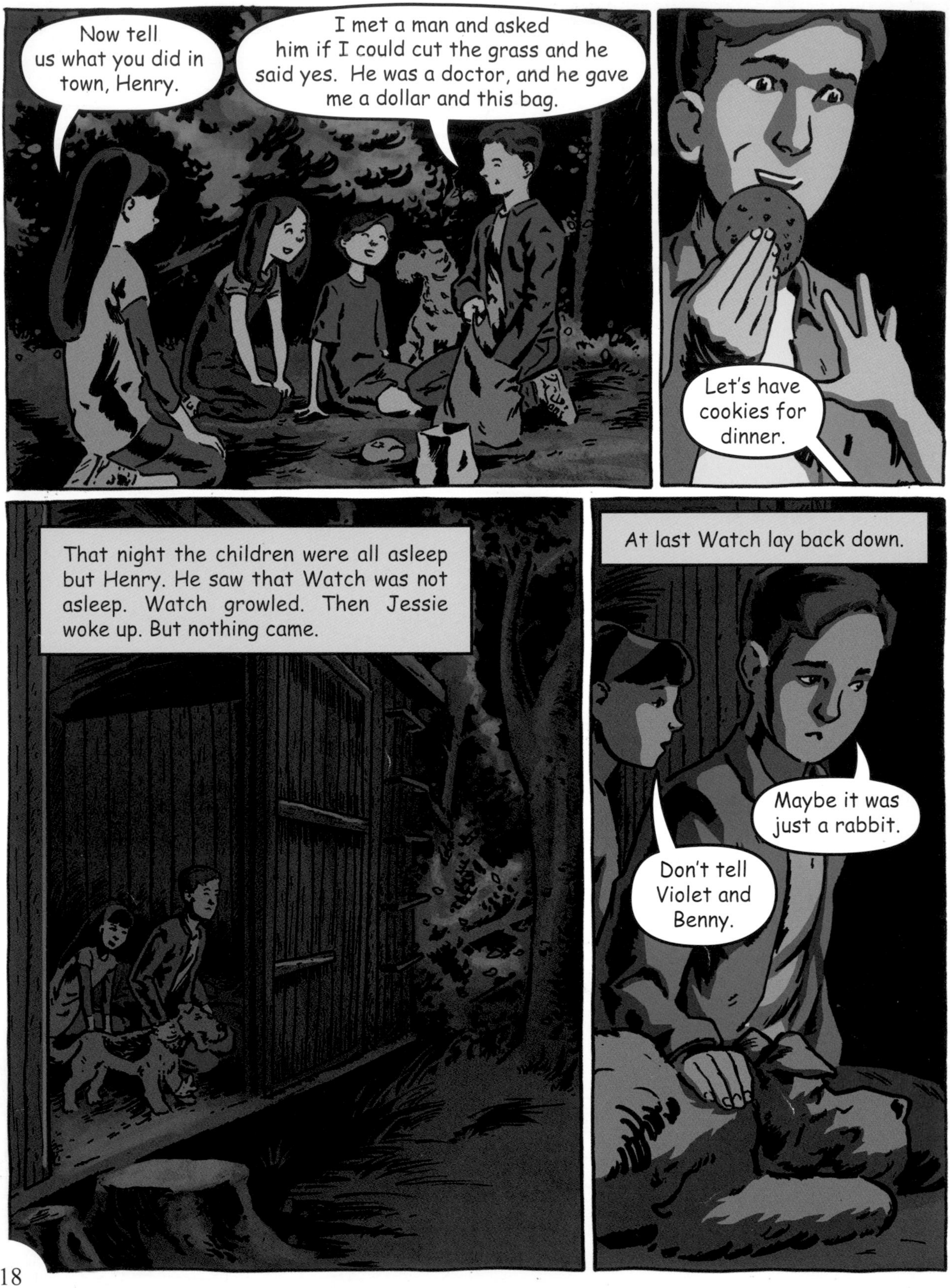
Now tell us what you did in town, Henry.
I met a man and asked him if I could cut the grass and he said yes. He was a doctor, and he gave me a dollar and this bag.
Let's have cookies for dinner.
That night the children were all asleep but Henry. He saw that Watch was not asleep. Watch growled. Then Jessie woke up. But nothing came.
At last Watch lay back down.
Maybe it was just a rabbit.
Don't tell Violet and Benny.

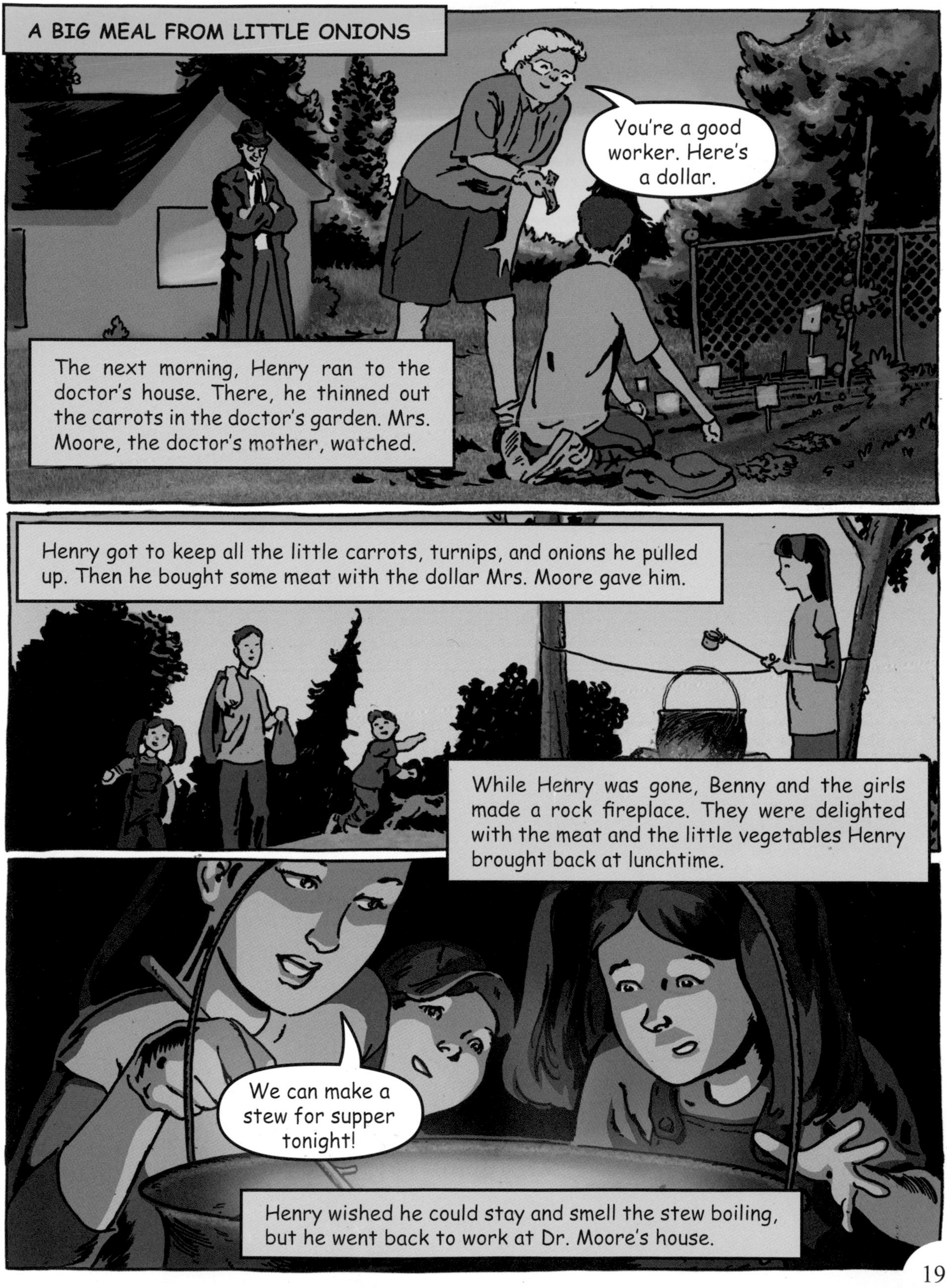
A BIG MEAL FROM LITTLE ONIONS
You're a good worker. Here's a dollar.
The next morning, Henry ran to the doctor's house. There, he thinned out the carrots in the doctor's garden. Mrs. Moore, the doctor's mother, watched.
Henry got to keep all the little carrots, turnips, and onions he pulled up. Then he bought some meat with the dollar Mrs. Moore gave him.
While Henry was gone, Benny and the girls made a rock fireplace. They were delighted with the meat and the little vegetables Henry brought back at lunchtime.
We can make a stew for supper tonight!
Henry wished he could stay and smell the stew boiling, but he went back to work at Dr. Moore's house.

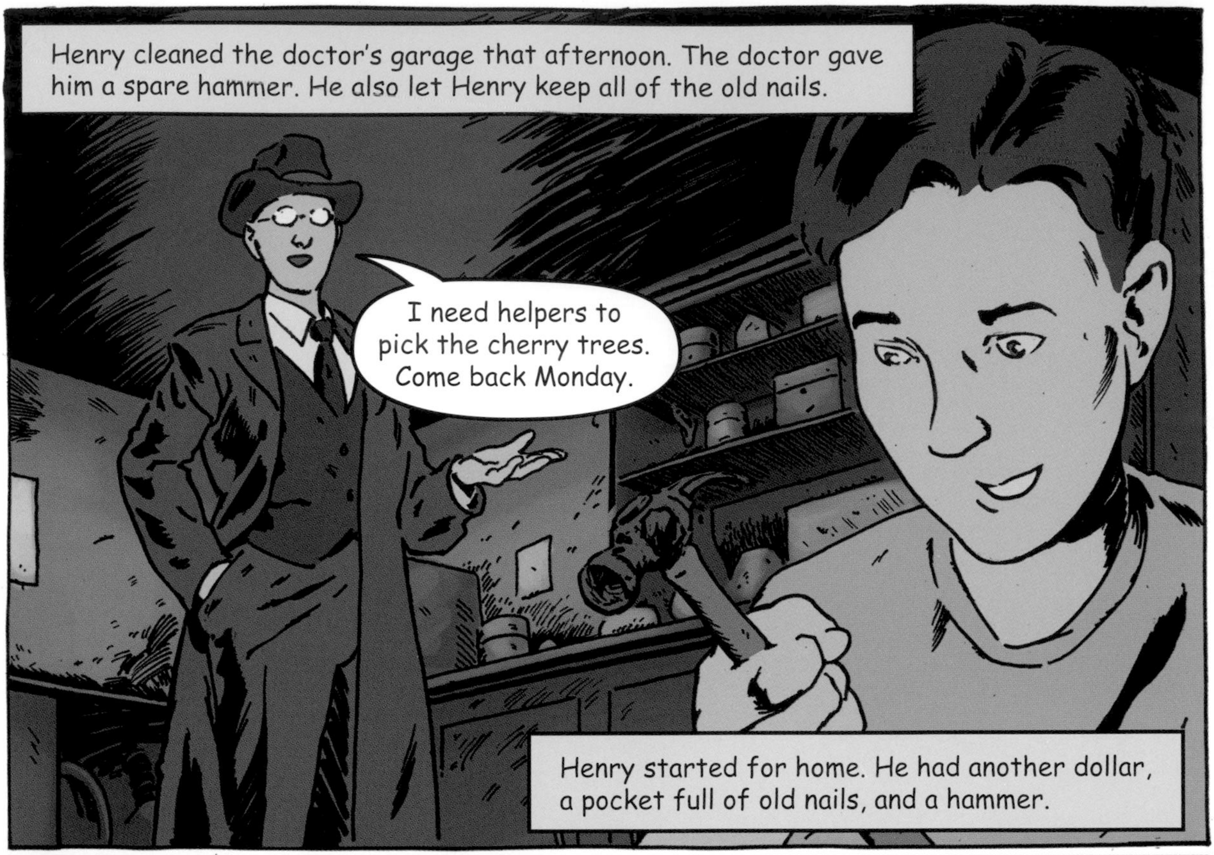
Henry cleaned the doctor's garage that afternoon. The doctor gave him a spare hammer. He also let Henry keep all of the old nails.
I need helpers to pick the cherry trees. Come back Monday.
Henry started for home. He had another dollar, a pocket full of old nails, and a hammer.

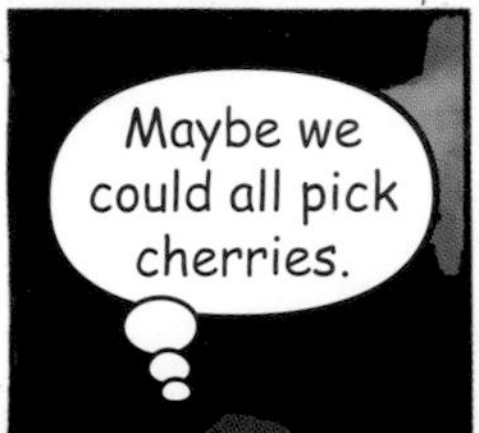
Maybe we could all pick cherries.

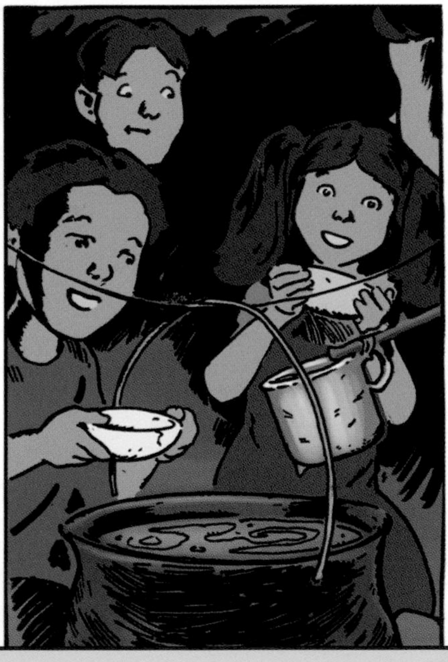
For dinner, Jessie ladled out the stew into plates and bowls. The meat was well cooked, and the vegetables were delicious.

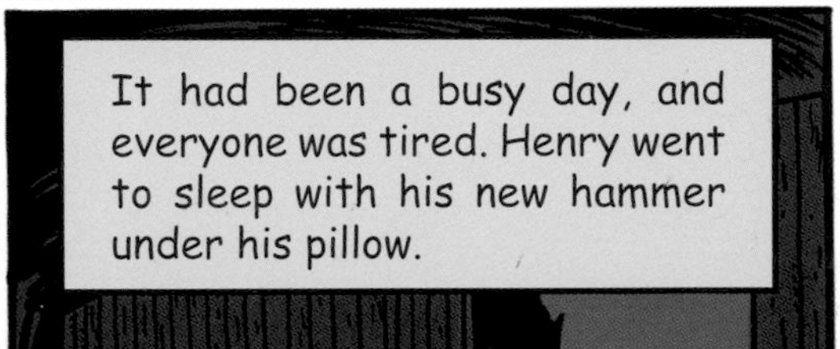
It had been a busy day, and everyone was tired. Henry went to sleep with his new hammer under his pillow.

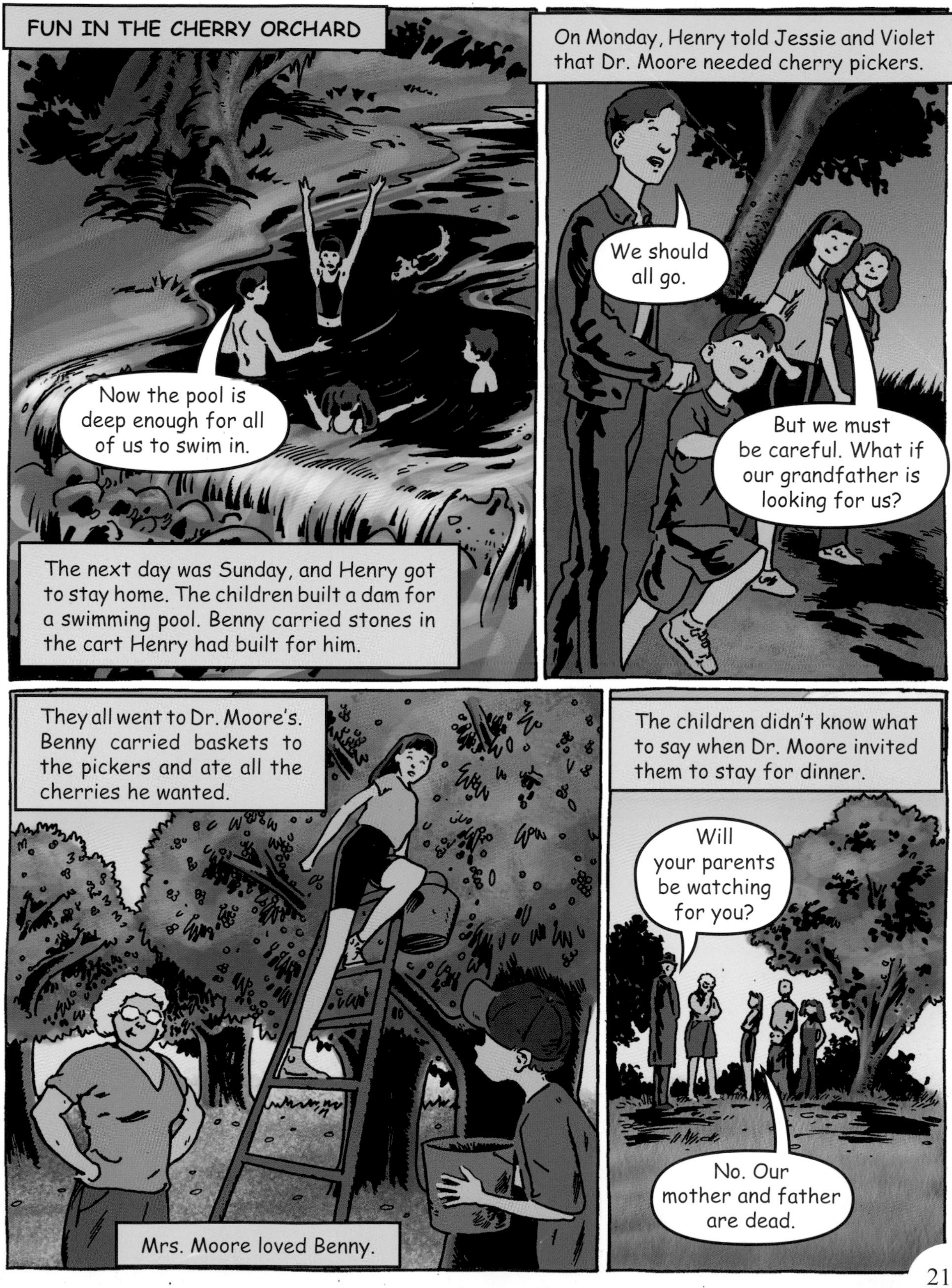
FUN IN THE CHERRY ORCHARD
Now the pool is deep enough for all of us to swim in.
The next day was Sunday, and Henry got to stay home. The children built a dam for a swimming pool. Benny carried stones in the cart Henry had built for him.
On Monday, Henry told Jessie and Violet that Dr. Moore needed cherry pickers.
We should all go.
But we must be careful. What if our grandfather is looking for us?
They all went to Dr. Moore's. Benny carried baskets to the pickers and ate all the cherries he wanted.
Mrs. Moore loved Benny.
The children didn't know what to say when Dr. Moore invited them to stay for dinner.
Will your parents be watching for you?
No. Our mother and father are dead.

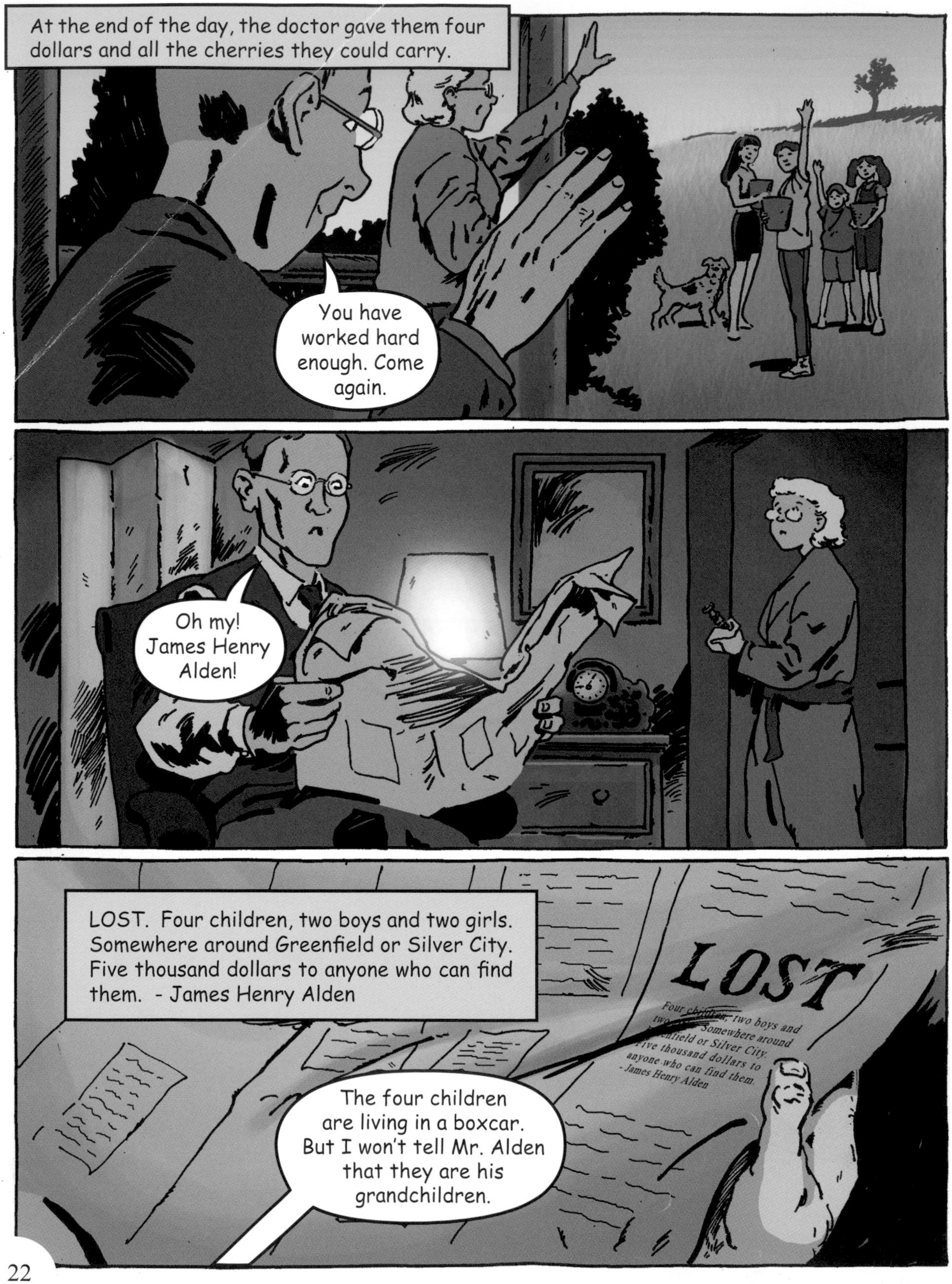
At the end of the day, the doctor gave them four dollars and all the cherries they could carry.
You have worked hard enough. Come again.
Oh my! James Henry Alden!
LOST. Four children, two boys and two girls. Somewhere around Greenfield or Silver City. Five thousand dollars to anyone who can find them. - James Henry Alden
LOST
The four children are living in a boxcar. But I won't tell Mr. Alden that they are his grandchildren.

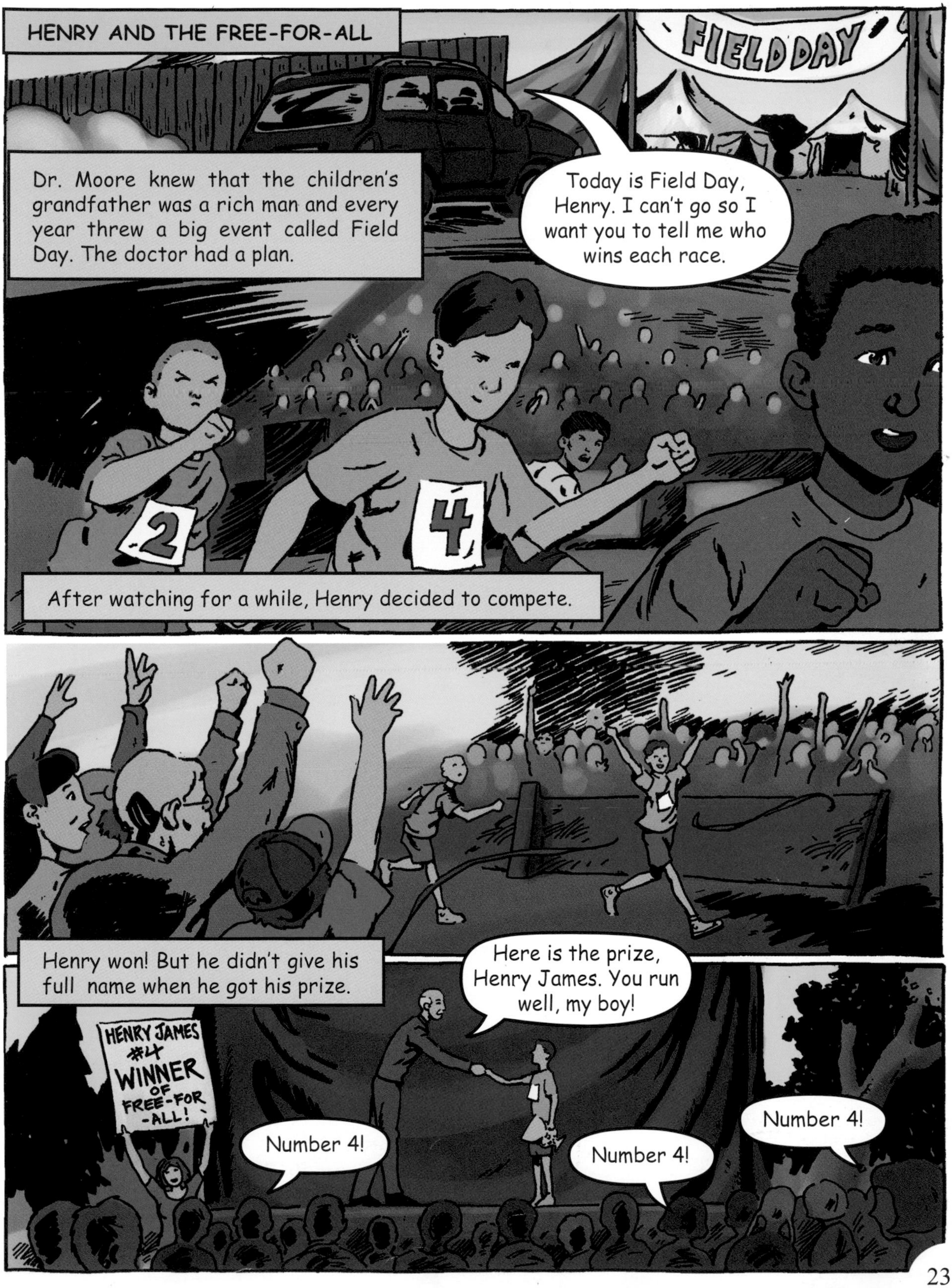
HENRY AND THE FREE-FOR-ALL
FIELD DAY
Dr. Moore knew that the children's grandfather was a rich man and every year threw a big event called Field Day. The doctor had a plan.
Today is Field Day, Henry. I can't go so I want you to tell me who wins each race.
2
4
After watching for a while, Henry decided to compete.
Henry won! But he didn't give his full name when he got his prize.
Here is the prize, Henry James. You run well, my boy!
HENRY JAMES #4 WINNER OF FREE-FOR -ALL!
Number 4!
Number 4!
Number 4!

THE DOCTOR TAKES A HAND

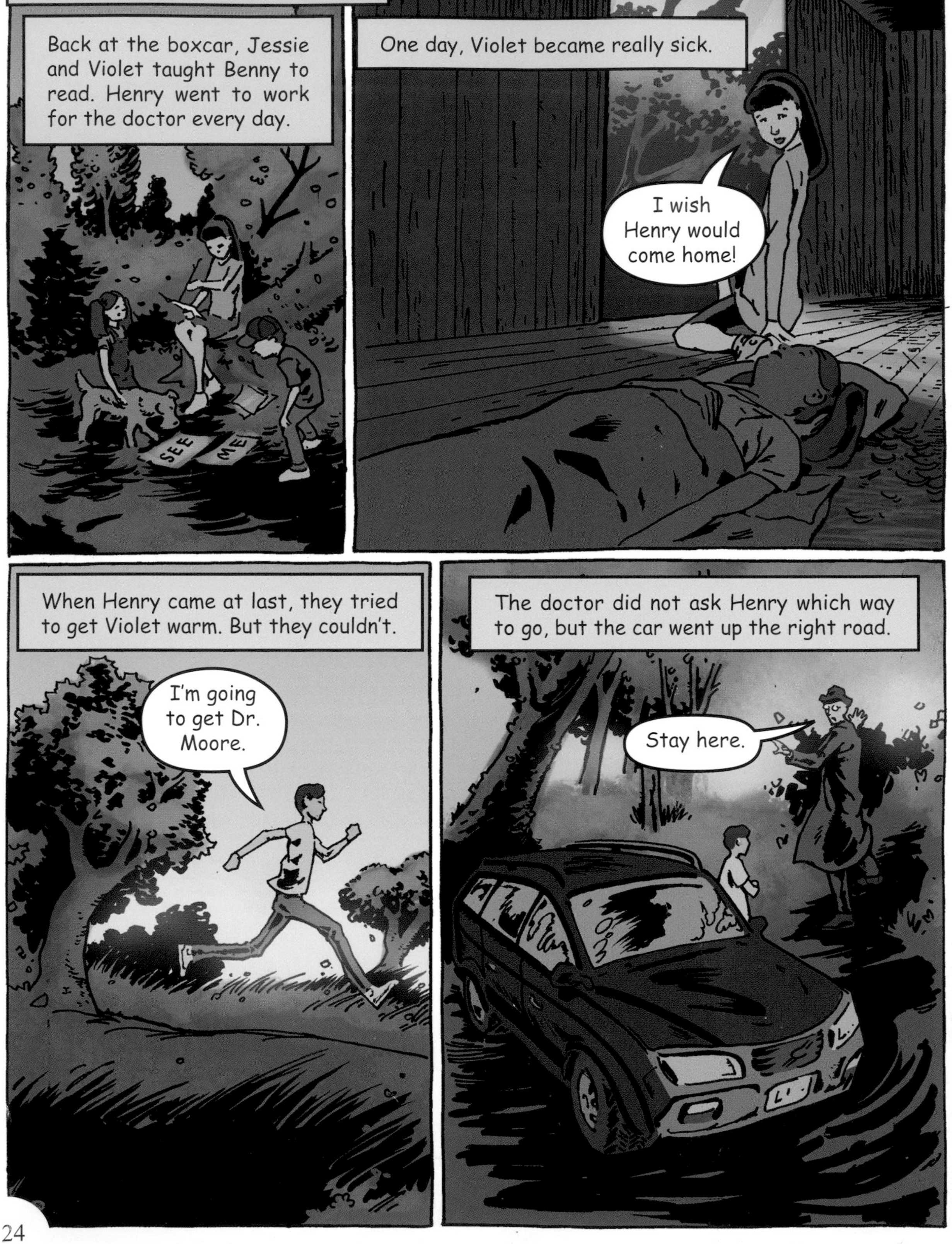
Back at the boxcar, Jessie and Violet taught Benny to read. Henry went to work for the doctor every day.
SEE
ME
One day, Violet became really sick.
I wish Henry would come home!
When Henry came at last, they tried to get Violet warm. But they couldn't.
I'm going to get Dr. Moore.
The doctor did not ask Henry which way to go, but the car went up the right road.
Stay here.

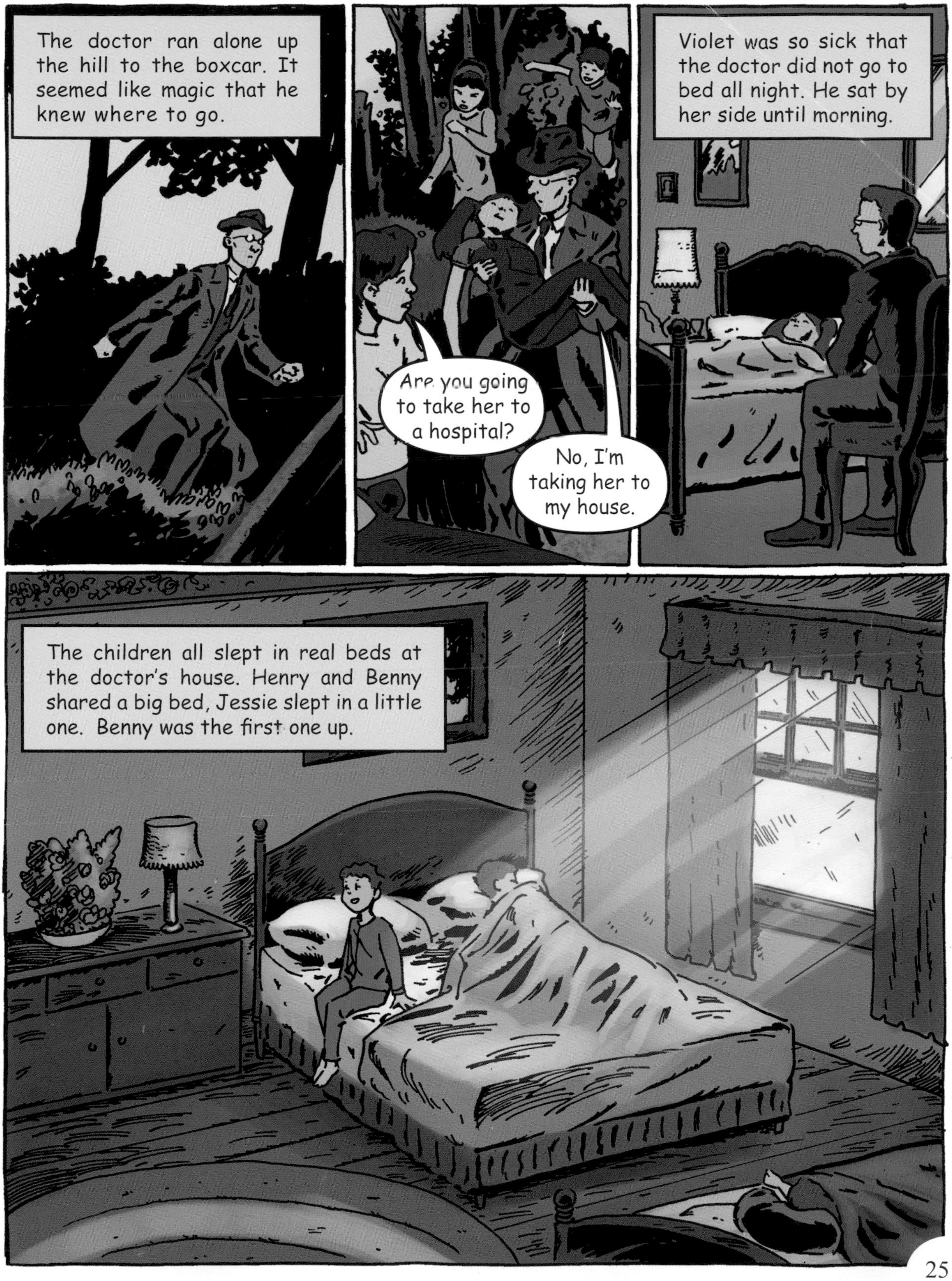
The doctor ran alone up the hill to the boxcar. It seemed like magic that he knew where to go.
Are you going to take her to a hospital?
No, I'm taking her to my house.
Violet was so sick that the doctor did not go to bed all night. He sat by her side until morning.
The children all slept in real beds at the doctor's house. Henry and Benny shared a big bed, Jessie slept in a little one. Benny was the first one up.

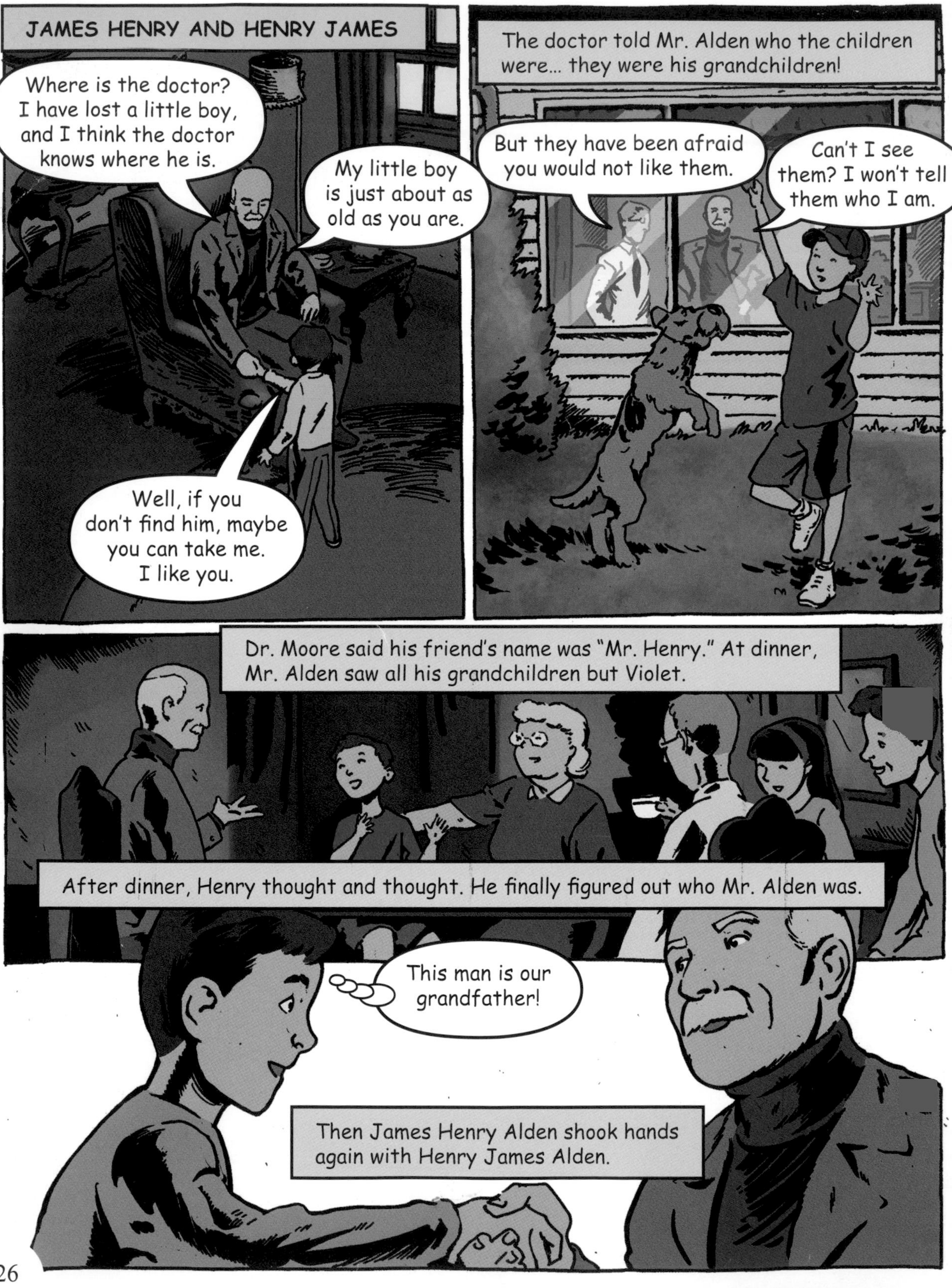
JAMES HENRY AND HENRY JAMES
Where is the doctor? I have lost a little boy, and I think the doctor knows where he is.
My little boy is just about as old as you are.
Well, if you don't find him, maybe you can take me. I like you.
The doctor told Mr. Alden who the children were... they were his grandchildren!
But they have been afraid you would not like them.
Can't I see them? I won't tell them who I am.
Dr. Moore said his friend's name was "Mr. Henry." At dinner, Mr. Alden saw all his grandchildren but Violet.
After dinner, Henry thought and thought. He finally figured out who Mr. Alden was.
This man is our grandfather!
Then James Henry Alden shook hands again with Henry James Alden.

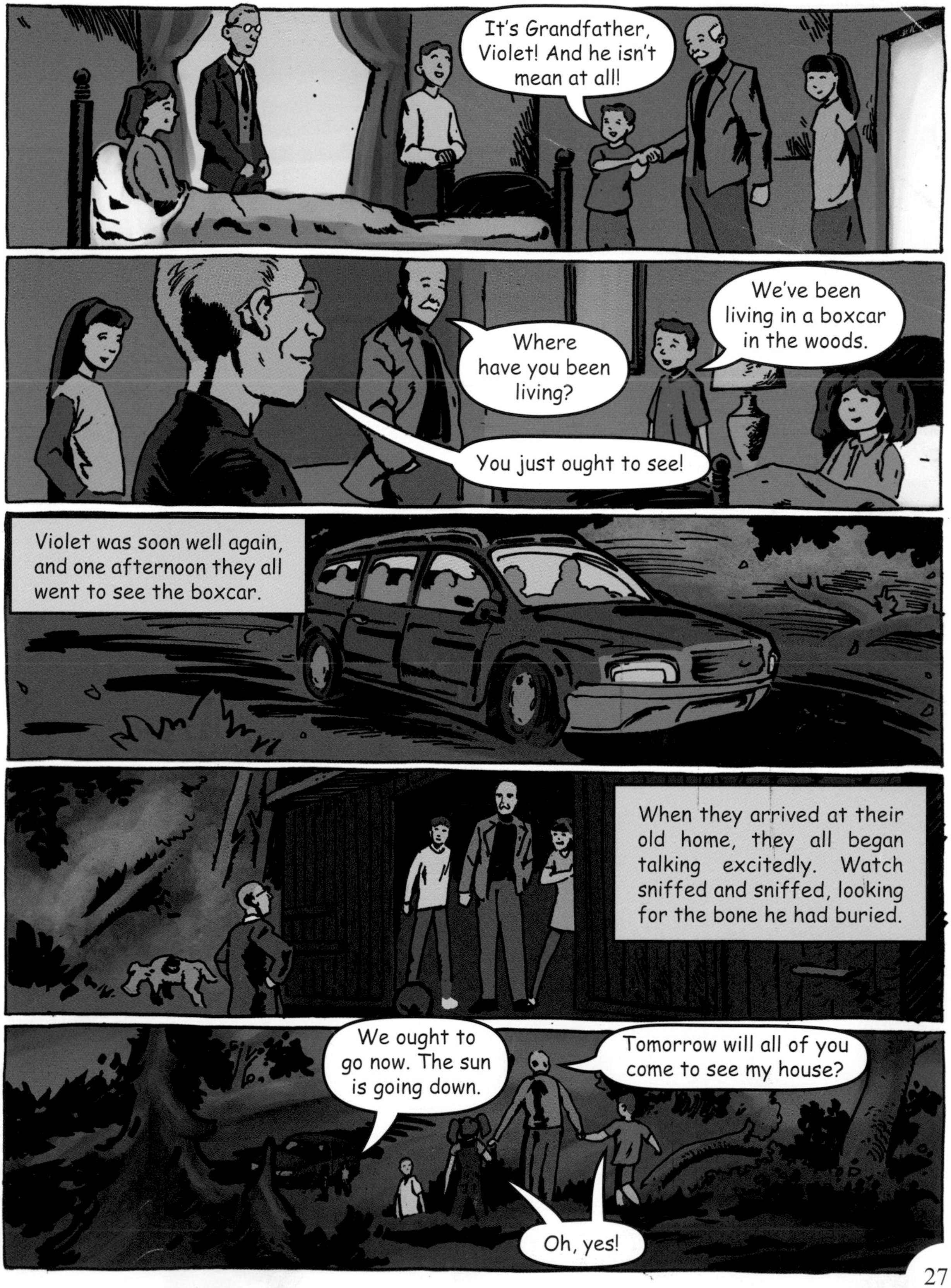
It's Grandfather, Violet! And he isn't mean at all!
Where have you been living?
We've been living in a boxcar in the woods.
You just ought to see!
Violet was soon well again, and one afternoon they all went to see the boxcar.
When they arrived at their old home, they all began talking excitedly. Watch sniffed and sniffed, looking for the bone he had buried.
We ought to go now. The sun is going down.
Tomorrow will all of you come to see my house?
Oh, yes!

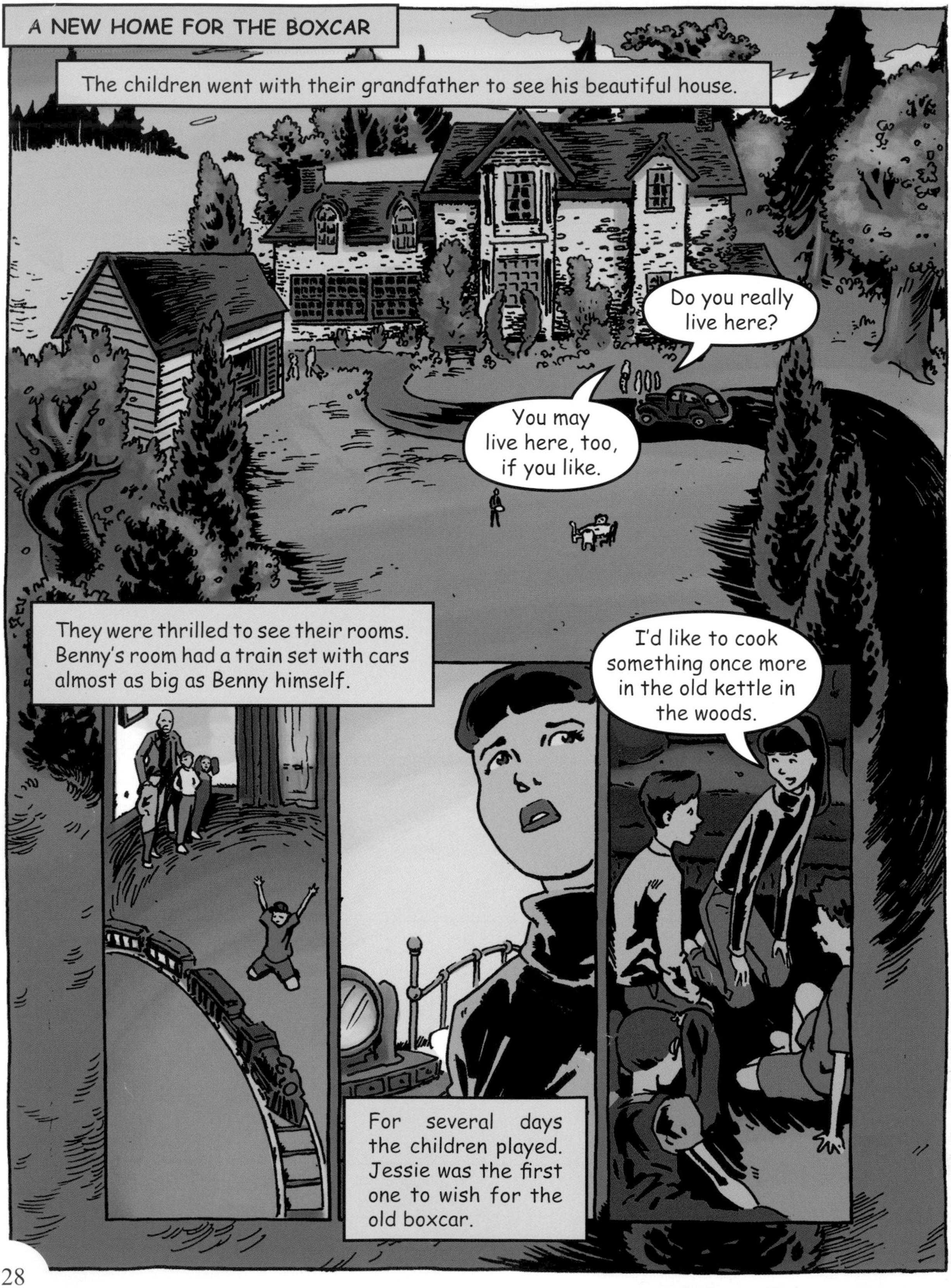
A NEW HOME FOR THE BOXCAR
The children went with their grandfather to see his beautiful house.
Do you really live here?
You may live here, too, if you like.
They were thrilled to see their rooms. Benny's room had a train set with cars almost as big as Benny himself.
I'd like to cook something once more in the old kettle in the woods.
For several days the children played. Jessie was the first one to wish for the old boxcar.

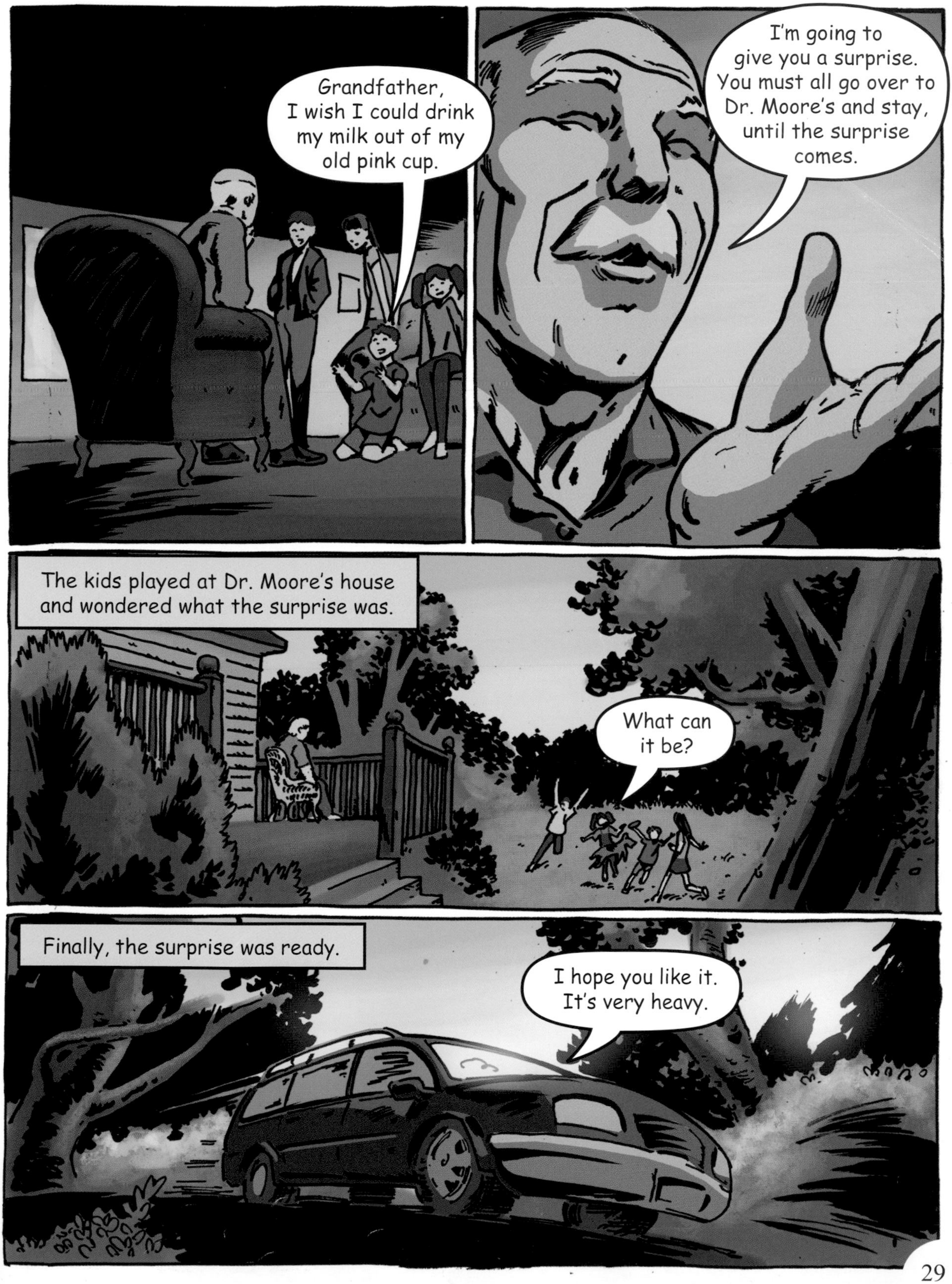
Grandfather, I wish I could drink my milk out of my old pink cup.
I'm going to give you a surprise. You must all go over to Dr. Moore's and stay, until the surprise comes.
The kids played at Dr. Moore's house and wondered what the surprise was.
What can it be?
Finally, the surprise was ready.
I hope you like it. It's very heavy.

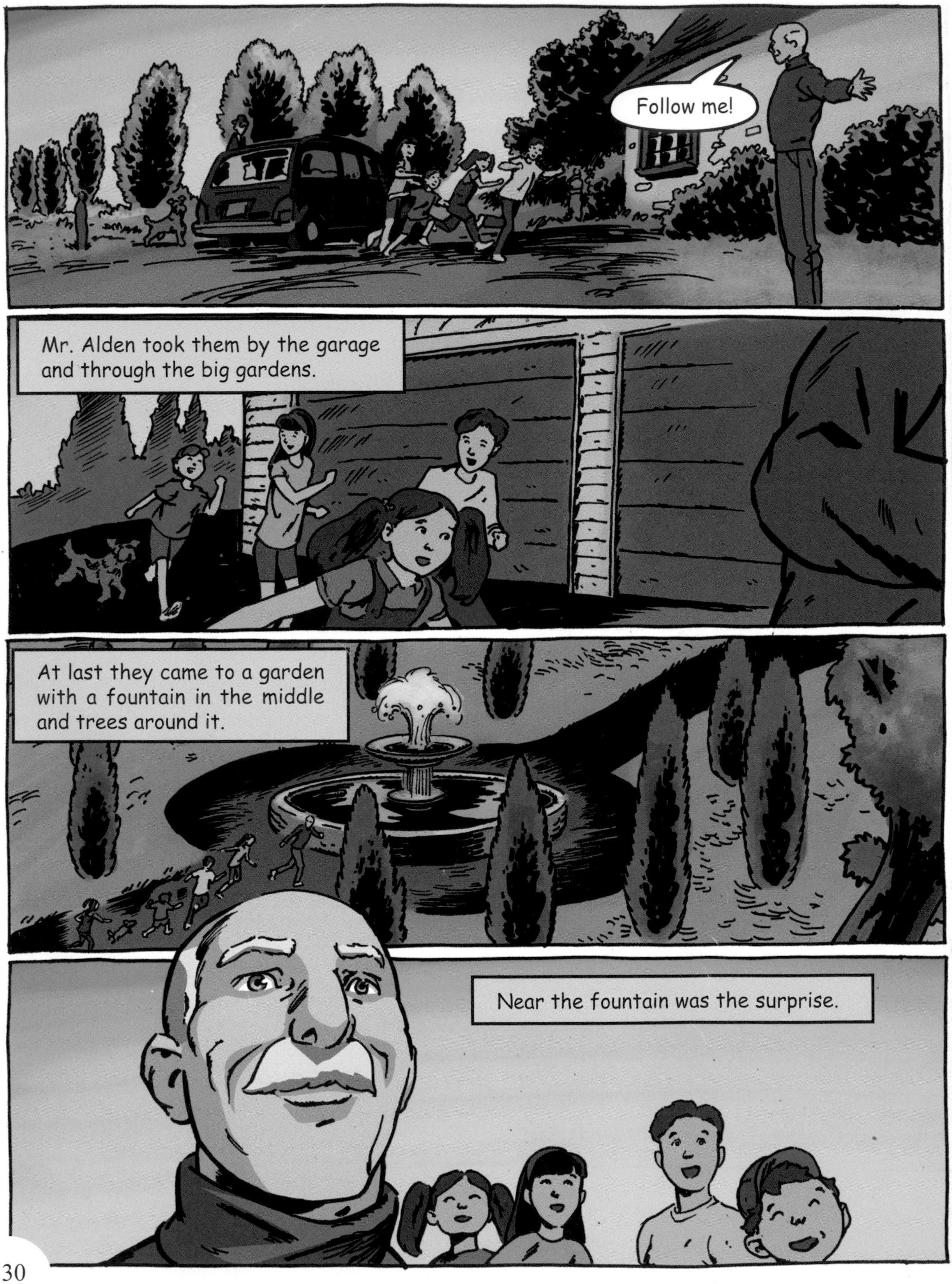
Follow me!
Mr. Alden took them by the garage and through the big gardens.
At last they came to a garden with a fountain in the middle and trees around it.
Near the fountain was the surprise.

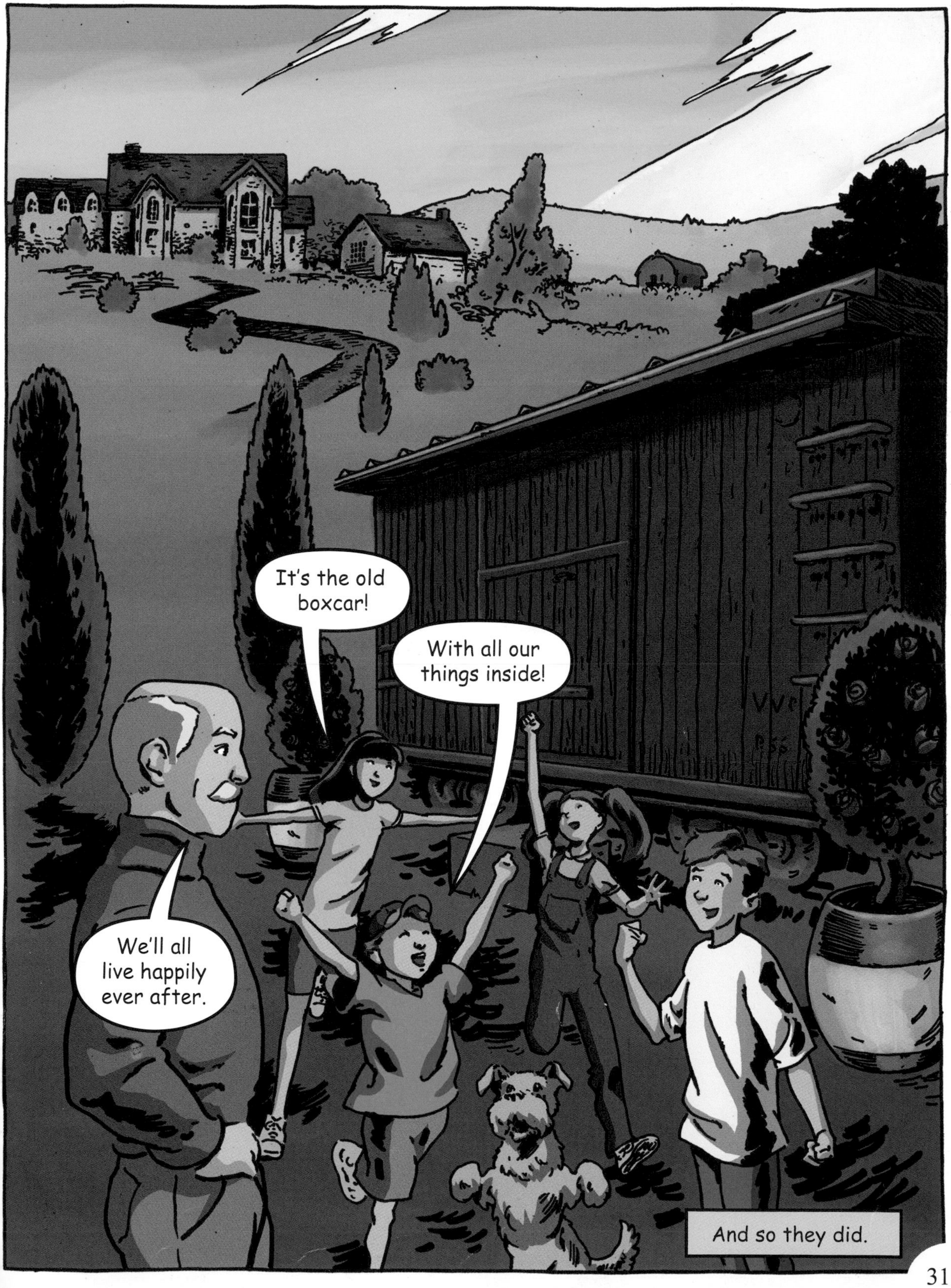
It's the old boxcar!
With all our things inside!
We'll all live happily ever after.
And so they did.

ABOUT THE CREATOR

Gertrude Chandler Warner was born on April 16, 1890, in Putnam, Connecticut. In 1918, Warner began teaching at Israel Putnam School. As a teacher, she discovered that many readers who liked an exciting story could not find books that were both easy and fun to read. She decided to try to meet this need. In 1942, *The Boxcar Children* was published for these readers.

Warner drew on her own experience to write *The Boxcar Children*. As a child she spent hours watching trains go by on the tracks near her family home. She often dreamed about what it would be like to live in a caboose or freight car—just as the Alden children do.

When readers asked for more Alden adventures, Warner began additional stories. While the mystery element is central to each of the books, she never thought of them as strictly juvenile mysteries. She liked to stress the Aldens' independence. Henry, Jessie, Violet, and Benny go about most of their adventures with as little adult supervision as possible—something that delights young readers.

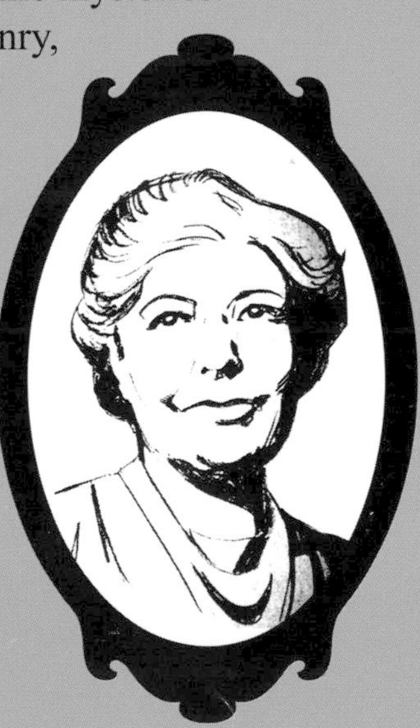

During her lifetime, Warner received hundreds of letters from fans as she continued the Aldens' adventures, writing nineteen Boxcar Children books in all. After her death in 1979, her publisher, Albert Whitman and Company, carried on Warner's vision. Today, the Boxcar Children series has more than 100 books.